YO-BCU-109

Then I remembered about the divorce.

Mommy and Daddy were getting one. Things were going to be different. We wouldn't live with Daddy anymore.

Mommy and I were staying at Nana and Granddaddy Gray's house "just for a while."

Then we were going to get our own house.

But before that, I was going to stay at Mama and Papa Brown's house.

That's a lot of houses!

Other books by Sharon Dennis Wyeth:

Always My Dad
Vampire Bugs: Stories Conjured from the Past
The World of Daughter McGuire
The Pen Pal series
Annie K's Theater

GINGER BROWN:
Too Many Houses

by Sharon Dennis Wyeth

illustrated by Cornelius Van Wright
and Ying-Hwa Hu

A FIRST STEPPING STONE BOOK

Random House 🏠 New York

For Georgia and Sims and our new house

Text copyright © 1996 by Sharon Dennis Wyeth
Illustrations copyright © 1996 by Cornelius Van Wright and Ying-Hwa Hu
All rights reserved under International and Pan-American Copyright
Conventions. Published in the United States by Random House, Inc., New York,
and simultaneously in Canada by Random House of Canada Limited, Toronto.

Library of Congress Cataloging-in-Publication Data
Wyeth, Sharon Dennis. Ginger Brown: too many houses / by Sharon
Dennis Wyeth. p. cm. "A First stepping stone book."
SUMMARY: When her parents get a divorce, six-year-old Ginger lives for a while
with each set of grandparents and begins to understand her mixed background
and her new family situation.
ISBN 0-679-85437-1 (pbk.) — ISBN 0-679-95437-6 (lib. bdg.)
[1. Divorce—Fiction. 2. Interracial marriage—Fiction. 3. Grandparents—
Fiction.] I. Title.
PZ7.W9746Gi 1995 [Fic]—dc20 94-23299

Printed in the United States of America
10 9 8 7 6 5 4 3 2 1
Random House, Inc. New York, Toronto, London, Sydney, Auckland

Contents

GINGER BROWN:
Too Many Houses

1
January

I was inside my house.

I was looking for my kitten.

I had my winter jacket on.

"Here, Leo! Here, Leo!" I called.

The suitcase was packed. Mommy was waiting at the front door. But I couldn't leave without Leo.

I looked under my bed. I saw one of my socks. I saw Leo's little red ball.

But I didn't see Leo.

So I ran up the stairs to the attic. The attic is where Leo and I like to hide.

"Here, kitty!" I called.

I looked in the corner behind my old crib. I looked inside the big box by the window. It was full of baby toys. My old blankie was right on top. Then I heard Mommy calling me.

"Ginger! The taxi is here! Come down, Ginger! We have to go!"

I ran down from the attic to my room. I looked for Leo underneath my quilt.

I ran into the bathroom and looked in the bathtub.

I passed my parents' room and looked on top of the dresser.

Leo wasn't anywhere!

"Hurry, sweetheart!" Mommy called.

I ran downstairs to the living room. Mommy was standing in the doorway. She was holding the big blue suitcase. She had packed my toothbrush and teddy bear in there.

We were going away for a very long time. To the city, where Nana and Granddaddy Gray live in an apartment.

Outside a car horn was honking.

Maybe Leo is asleep in the kitchen! I thought. *He likes to sleep under the stove.*

I ran toward the kitchen, but Mommy caught me.

"Come on, sweetheart," she said.

"But…but what about Leo?"

Mommy hugged me. "We have to leave Leo for now. Let's go."

We went out of my house. Snow was on the front porch. A yellow taxi was parked at the curb.

"Leo will be okay. Daddy will be with him," Mommy said.

I asked, "Isn't Daddy coming too?"

Mommy's face was sad. "Daddy isn't coming with us. Remember?"

We got inside the taxi while the driver put the suitcase in the trunk.

The driver got in the taxi and started the motor. Then I remembered about the divorce. Mommy and Daddy were getting one. Things were going to be different. We wouldn't live with Daddy anymore.

Mommy opened up her pocketbook and gave me a stick of chewing gum. But I didn't feel like chewing.

The taxi was going fast.

I looked out the window.

My house was gone.

February

Nana was sitting in her chair. She had on her glasses. She was watching the news.

Granddaddy Gray was in his chair. He had on glasses, too. He was reading the paper.

I was sitting on the windowsill. I was looking out the window.

"Sit on the couch, Ginger," said Nana. "It makes me nervous to see you sitting on the windowsill."

Then she said, "Why don't you make

valentines?" But I didn't want to make dumb valentines.

"Ever since you got home from school, you've been staring out that window," Nana said. "Come over and sit on my lap."

But I was much too grumpy to sit on anyone's lap. I wanted to sit on the windowsill. Next to the plant.

I liked looking out the window. The people down below were small, like ants.

I could see the post office.

I could see the bus stop.

I could count yellow taxis, too. I counted ten go by.

I kept thinking: *Maybe Daddy is in one of those taxis.* But deep down I knew that Daddy wasn't going to visit me today.

Leo wasn't going to visit me either. Leo could never visit! Because of that dumb rule in Nana and Granddaddy Gray's apartment building. The rule that said No Pets.

I counted two more taxis. That made eleven and twelve.

If Mommy and I stayed here forever, I thought, *I might count a million.*

But Mommy and I were staying at Nana and Granddaddy Gray's house "just for a while."

Then we were going to get our own house.

But before that, I was going to stay at Mama and Papa Brown's house.

That's a lot of houses!

Mama and Papa Brown are Daddy's parents.

Their name is Brown. But their skin isn't brown.

Mama and Papa Brown's skin looks pinkish white. Like Daddy's.

And Nana and Granddaddy Gray are not really gray.

Their skin is brown. Like Mommy's.

My last name is Brown too, but I'm tan!

Sometimes I wonder what the reason is for all of this.

Granddaddy Gray got up from his chair. He took my hand and we walked to the couch.

"I'm going to show you something," he said. "You'll like it." He went and got the big black picture album. Then he sat down beside me and opened it up.

There were lots of pictures of Mommy. When Mommy was six years old, just like me.

"Wasn't your mommy cute?" asked Granddaddy Gray.

"No," I said, and turned away.

I used to like those pictures. But not anymore.

Nana looked at me and shook her head.

"My, what a face!" she said. "What can we do to cheer you up?"

"How about making a valentine for your daddy?" asked Granddaddy Gray.

"Unh-unh," I said.

Daddy wasn't here, so how could I give it to him?

Nana brought over some red paper and glue.

"How about a nice pretty one for Mommy?" she said.

She cut out a big red heart and put it in my hand. She showed me a box of colored sparkles.

"You can glue sparkles on it," she said.

"Unh-unh," I said.

Nana stroked my hair. My hair is bouncy. Just like Nana's. Just like Mommy's.

"A nice valentine from you might cheer your mommy up," Nana said.

"No," I said.

I was mad.

Mommy made us leave our house. She made us leave Daddy and Leo.

"I don't feel like making valentines," I said.

"How about helping me set the table?" asked Nana. "Your mommy will be home from work soon."

"I don't know how to set the table," I told her.

"Then Granddaddy and I will teach you," said Nana.

Just then the door opened and Mommy came in.

"Hi, everybody!" she said.

She came over and hugged me.

"This is for you, sweetheart." She

handed me an envelope that was shaped like a heart.

Inside was a valentine.

Just for me!

A great big one!

That made me glad.

But when I didn't have one for Mommy…that made me sad.

3
March

"I'm going to teach you how to fly this," said Daddy.

It was a red kite.

The wind was blowing. Daddy had come for a visit. We had gone to the park.

Daddy ran across the grass with the kite. I ran after him. The kite went up in the air. He put the ball of string in my hand.

"Hold on tight!" he told me.

I held on tight. The kite kept going up

higher and higher! The string was unwinding faster and faster. I got scared.

"Will it come back?" I asked Daddy.

"Sure, honey," he said.

But the wind kept tugging at the string. My new kite was so high, I almost couldn't see it.

"Help!" I said.

Daddy helped me hold the string. He was winding it up. "We'll bring the kite back," he said.

He kept winding up the string. The kite got closer. But suddenly the wind stopped blowing. My kite took a dive and landed in a tall, skinny tree.

"I told you it wasn't coming back," I said.

But Daddy tugged and tugged, until the kite jerked loose. I ran over and picked it up off the grass.

Daddy said, "Maybe that's enough of kites for one day. Maybe we should look at clouds instead."

Daddy sat on a bench and I sat on his knee. We looked up at the blue sky. I was the first one to see a cloud that looked like something else.

"My cloud looks like a tiger!" I said. I pointed it out to Daddy.

Daddy gave me a kiss and pointed out his cloud too. "My cloud looks like…a piano!" he said.

After we looked at clouds, Daddy opened his knapsack. He took out my quilt. Mommy and I had left a lot of my things behind in the old house.

"Did you bring anything else?" I asked.

"Mommy will get the rest of your things," said Daddy. Then he told me that somebody else was going to live in my old house. Then he said, "I have to go away for a while."

I got a big gulp in my throat. "Where are you going?"

"The band is doing a big tour. Texas, Louisiana, Florida."

The gulp in my throat got bigger.

Daddy's job is playing the trumpet in a jazz band. His band is always traveling to interesting places.

I think he goes on the road too much. And so does Mommy.

"I'll miss you so much!" said Daddy.

A tear came out of my eye. I already missed him, because we didn't live together. When he goes on the road, we couldn't even visit.

Daddy gave me his handkerchief.

"Spring is pretty much here," he said.

"Soon it will be summer. Then you'll be on the farm. At Papa and Mama Brown's house. Won't that be fun?"

"That's too many houses!" I said. "And anyway, what about Leo? While you're on the road, where's Leo going to live?"

"He'll stay with the Cromwells," said Daddy. "The Cromwells like Leo. They'll take good care of him."

The Cromwells lived next door to our old house.

I started to cry. "You gave Leo away!" I said. "I don't like you."

I slid off Daddy's knee and sat down on the bench.

"Shh, don't cry," Daddy said.

He put his arm around me. He started to sing our song. A song he made up for me, called "Sweet Ginger Brown."

"Stop that silly singing!" I said.

We went back to Nana and Grand-daddy Gray's building. We went up to the apartment in the elevator. Granddaddy Gray was waiting for us at the door. Daddy gave him my kite.

Daddy bent down and kissed me good-bye. I felt his scratchy beard on my cheek. Then he waved and got back into the elevator. I ran into the apartment, to look out the window.

In a few minutes, I saw Daddy walk out of the building. Down below, he looked very small. I waved and waved, but Daddy didn't look up at me.

Granddaddy Gray touched my shoulder. "Come have a snack, Ginger. You can have milk and cookies."

I went into the kitchen. Granddaddy put some cookies on a plate. He poured me a glass of milk. I tried to sing a song. The song that belonged to Daddy and me—"Sweet Ginger Brown."

But I couldn't.

Only Daddy knew the words.

4
April

It was raining. I was in school. Grand-daddy Gray drives me there every morning. My teacher told us to draw a picture of something we like very much.

I drew a picture of a kitten. He had orange fur and green eyes. He looked like Leo.

Leo was so little. I wonder if he remembers me. I used to wrap him up in my blankie. I used to put him in my wagon and pull him around.

I remember Leo. He liked to play with a little red ball.

When he licked my cheek, his tongue felt like sandpaper.

5
May

Nana and I were making pie.

Nana let me cut the butter for the crust. I cut the butter in little pieces with a real knife. All by myself.

"Did Mommy like to make pie, when she was a little girl?" I asked.

"Oh yes," said Nana. "When I could get her to sit still, that is!"

Nana said to dump the butter into the bowl with the flour. I did and mixed it all up. But not with a spoon. With my fingers.

"Mommy didn't sit still?" I asked.

"Not very often," said Nana. "Your mommy's favorite thing to do was to run around."

Nana poured a little water on top of the flour. She told me to make a big ball out of the dough.

"Around and around this little apartment," said Nana. "Up and down the hall. On the sidewalk, in the park. Your mommy loved to run."

I could not remember ever seeing Mommy run.

Nana put the ball of dough I made onto the table. She told me to tap it with the rolling pin. Then she and I rolled the dough out. That was our crust.

We put the crust into the pie pan. We put the pie pan into the oven. The crust began to bake.

Then Nana gave me a bowl of straw-berries.

"Did Mommy like to eat strawberry pie when she was little?" I asked Nana.

Nana laughed. "Oh, she could sit still for the eating part."

While I pulled the green stems off the strawberries, Nana made a sauce with sugar. She stirred the sauce in a pan on

top of the stove. When the sauce was done, Nana put it in a bowl to cool.

Then, together, Nana and I sliced up the strawberries.

Granddaddy Gray came into the kitchen.

"Oh my! I smell pie! Who are you baking it for?"

"Ginger is the baker," said Nana. "I

think she should decide who will eat it."

I licked the strawberry juice off my fingers.

"Oh, Ginger," begged Granddaddy Gray. "I hope that pie is for me."

"I'm not sure," I said.

"Who is it for, then?" asked Granddaddy Gray.

"For somebody," I told him.

Granddaddy Gray went back to the living room.

"I hope that somebody saves me a piece," he called out.

Nana took the crust out of the oven. It was light brown.

"Can I put in the strawberries?" I asked.

"Not yet," said Nana. "We have to wait for the crust to cool."

Nana wiped off the kitchen table. She

looked at the strawberries I'd sliced. She smiled at me.

"Nothing makes a place feel more like home than a pie," she said.

"Is this my home now?" I asked her.

"This is your home whenever you want it to be," said Nana.

In a few minutes the crust was cool. I spooned the strawberries into the crust. It looked like a real pie! Nana poured the sweet sauce she had made on top of it.

I went into the living room.

"It's finished," I said.

Granddaddy Gray went into the kitchen.

I sat down on the windowsill, next to the plant. That plant was getting taller and taller.

I looked out the window. Sometimes I can see Mommy coming back from work.

Walking home from the bus stop.

"Here she comes!" I said.

Down on the street, Mommy looked tiny. But I could see her in her blue jacket.

I went to the kitchen and helped Granddaddy Gray set the table. Nana had put whipped cream on top of the pie!

Mommy came into the apartment. I heard her say, "Whew! What a day!"

I ran out of the kitchen and kissed her. She kissed me too. Right on my dimple. Mommy looked tired.

"Come here," I said.

Mommy came into the kitchen and I showed her the pie.

"Oh my!" Mommy said. "Strawberry pie! My favorite!"

"I made it," I said. "Just for you."

6
June

School was out. I was down on the farm. Where Mama and Papa Brown live. Where Daddy used to live, when he was a boy.

Mommy was still at Nana and Granddaddy Gray's. She had to stay in the city, so that she could go to her job at the magazine.

Papa Brown said he was glad I had come. He needed my help, doing some farm work.

"Can you handle it, Ginger girl?" he

asked. "There's a lot to do around here."

"I'm not sure," I answered. "I've never done any farm work."

"Well," he said, "I reckon you can learn."

First we went to the henhouse. My job was to gather the eggs.

I had to wear Mama Brown's old shoes. The ones she wears in the henhouse, because the floor in there gets so dirty.

The chickens made loud squawking noises when I went inside. I felt scared. But I still picked up the eggs and put them in my basket.

Next we went to the vegetable garden. I pulled some baby carrots out of the ground.

"We'll have those for dinner," said Papa Brown.

But I couldn't wait to taste one. So I
washed off one and had it for a snack.

Then I drank some water from the
hose. Farm work made me thirsty.

Papa Brown smiled at me.

"You're a good worker," he said.
"Now, let's go pick a few peaches."

Papa Brown and I walked to the peach
tree. The peach tree was tall. But Papa

Brown could reach the branches, because he was tall, too.

"Would you like to pick some?" he asked me.

"I can't reach," I said.

Papa Brown took my basket and put it in the shade. Then he stooped down low. "Climb on my shoulders."

I climbed on Papa Brown's shoulders. When Papa Brown stood up, I felt so big!

"Reckon you can reach now," he said.

I reached out and felt one of the peaches. It was soft and ripe. I gave it to Papa Brown and he put it in the pocket of his overalls.

"That one's for Mama Brown," he said. "Now, pick two more—one for you and one for me."

I found two more ripe ones and passed them down.

Papa Brown put me back down on the ground.

"I wish I were as big as you are," I said.

"You are big," said Papa Brown. "I bet you are very strong too. Show me your muscles."

I held up my arms and showed him my muscles.

Papa Brown chuckled. "Look at that! You're strong all right."

I looked up at him. His eyes are blue. Just like Daddy's. Just like mine.

He took one of the peaches out of his pocket and wiped it off.

"This one looks sweet," he said, giving it to me. "A sweet peach for my sweet Ginger girl."

I laughed and took a bite. The peach *was* sweet. The juice dripped down my chin. Papa Brown ate his peach too.

Then we took the third peach and the basket of eggs and carrots into the house and gave them to Mama Brown.

"You look hot," said Mama Brown. "Maybe it's time for a swim."

"Are you a swimmer?" Papa Brown asked me.

"No, sir," I said.

"Well, that's another thing you can learn," Papa Brown said. "Rustle up your bathing suit. We'll go to the pond."

I went to the room at the top of the stairs. It was Daddy's room when he was a boy. But it was going to be my room all summer.

I put on my bathing suit and went back downstairs. My bathing suit felt very tight.

"Guess you've grown some since the

last time you wore it," said Mama Brown.

Then she gave me her bathing cap and stuffed in my hair.

"Don't run Ginger ragged," Mama Brown warned Papa Brown. "After all, she just got here."

"Oh, she can handle it," Papa Brown said. "Don't worry about that Ginger girl. She's strong."

He looked at me and grinned. "Isn't that right?"

"Yes," I answered. "I am."

7
July

Mommy came to see me at the farm!

We went up to my room. She braided my hair.

I showed her my favorite peach tree from my window.

"I like that tree too," said Mommy. She hugged me.

"I missed you," I told her.

"Next time I see you," said Mommy, "I'll take you home. To our new place."

"What's the new place like?" I asked.

"It's an apartment on a quiet street," she said. "It's near a playground. The old owners are still living in it. But soon it will belong to us."

It was a bright sunny day.

"Let's go outside," I said.

Mommy said, "Okay, but first put on your shoes."

"But I don't wear shoes here in the country," I said. "Except when we go to church or collect eggs in the henhouse. And anyway—"

Mommy found my shoes under the bed.

"Let's just put these on," she said.

She tried to stuff my foot inside one shoe. But the shoe didn't fit anymore.

"Well, I'll be!" said Mommy.

"I tried to tell you," I said.

When we went outside, I had bare feet.

Mama Brown was fixing us supper. Papa Brown was putting the cows in the barn.

I took Mommy's hand.

"Let's run," I said.

"Run?" asked Mommy.

"Yes," I said. "You like running."

"I do?" said Mommy.

"Nana told me that when you were a little girl, you ran all over the place."

"Oh, Nana told you that, did she?"

"Nana said you couldn't sit still long enough to make a pie," I said.

Mommy laughed.

"Come on!" I tugged her hand.

She looked at her feet. She was wearing her dressy shoes.

"Guess I'll have to take these off," she said, laughing again.

Mommy kicked off her shoes and started to run.

"Hey, wait for me!" I cried. "We're supposed to be racing."

"Well, come on!" she said.

Mommy was fast!

But I was fast too.

I ran, and soon I caught up.

"Let's have a real race!" I said.

"Okay," she said. "First one to the peach tree—"

Mommy had a big smile on her face. I counted to three and we ran!

Mommy and I ran so fast. We touched the tree at the same time!

We both won!

8
August

Mama Brown was in the kitchen. I heard her banging jars. She was making blueberry jam.

And singing. In a loud voice with the radio.

I was sitting under the peach tree, doing nothing but looking at my toes. And then at a blade of grass. And then at a ladybug.

Mama Brown came outside wearing no shoes. I saw her pale and chubby toes.

Mama Brown bent down and picked a buttercup.

"Let's see if you like butter," said Mama Brown. She held the buttercup under my chin. "You do like butter!" she said.

I jumped up and picked my own buttercup.

"Let me try!"

I held the buttercup under Mama Brown's chin. A little yellow light shined under her face.

"You like butter too!" I said.

Mama Brown laughed and hugged me. Her arms are chubby too.

"Come on," she said. "Let's go get the mail."

I followed her around to the front of the house. The grass tickled my feet.

The mailbox was at the end of the

walk. Mama Brown opened the box and took out the mail.

"Here's one for you," she said.

She handed me a postcard. It had a picture of a river on the front.

I turned the postcard over. It was from Daddy! Next to his name, there were lots of xxx's. The xxx's were for the kisses he was sending me.

"Want me to read it to you?" asked Mama Brown.

I gave her the postcard. I can read, but not that well.

"The picture on the front is of the Mississippi River," said Mama Brown. "Your daddy is in a place called New Orleans playing his trumpet."

"What did Daddy write?" I asked.

"Dear Ginger," read Mama Brown. "New Orleans is an exciting city, filled with music. I hope I can bring you here someday. This morning I saw a big cloud that looked just like an elephant. It even had a trunk. I hope you are having a wonderful summer. I miss you very much and can't wait until my tour is over. Love, Daddy."

"Isn't that nice?" said Mama Brown.

"Very nice," I said. "Very, *very* nice."

"There's more," said Mama Brown. "He's scribbled something at the bottom.

"P.S.," she read, "I heard from the Cromwells. They have moved to Florida and taken Leo with them. They love cats. We're lucky that Leo is with such a good family."

"What!" I said.

I took Daddy's postcard and threw it down on the ground.

"First he gives Leo away! Then he lets the Cromwells take him to Florida! Leo could have been here on the farm."

"What a shame that nobody thought of that," said Mama Brown.

Mama Brown picked up Daddy's postcard. We walked to the front porch.

"Leo is only a kitten," I said. "He's lonely without me."

Mama Brown sat down on the porch swing. She pulled me onto her lap.

"How about you?" asked Mama Brown.

"Are you lonely here on the farm?"

I was. Kind of. Now there wasn't just Daddy to miss. There was Mommy and Nana and Grandaddy Gray, too.

"Don't be lonely," said Mama Brown. "You have Papa Brown and me. Just like Leo has the Cromwells."

I leaned back against Mama Brown. Mama Brown's lap is soft. Her lap is big enough for a kid my size.

"Your Daddy used to sit on my lap," she said.

"Is Daddy lonely?" I asked.

"Of course he is. Far away from you, going from city to city. And I'm sure he's very sorry about your kitten.

"Why don't you have a cool drink of water?" said Mama Brown. "And then find something to do."

"Okay," I said.

We went into the house, where I had a drink. I put Daddy's postcard upstairs in my room. Then I brought my paints outside.

I sat down under the peach tree. I painted a picture.

I painted a picture of the white house and the red barn. I painted a yellow buttercup. I painted a sky with a cloud that looked like a trumpet.

My picture was just like a postcard.

I would send it to Daddy. Maybe.

One week later, the telephone rang.

Brring!

I picked up the phone. When the phone rings, Mama Brown always lets me answer it.

"Hello," I said.

"Hello, honey," said a familiar voice.

"Hi, Daddy!" I said. "Are you calling long-distance?"

"Yes, I am," he said.

"Your voice doesn't sound far away."

"That's because I talk so loud, I guess." Daddy laughed his same old laugh.

"Thanks for the painting you sent me," he said.

"You're welcome," I said. "How's it going?"

"Okay, I guess."

"Are you lonely?" I asked.

"Well, I miss you," said Daddy.

"I wish I could see you," I said. "Do the people like it when you play the trumpet?"

"They like it okay. How about you?" said Daddy. "Having fun on the farm?"

"I can swim now," I said.

"You can? No kidding!" Daddy's voice sounded excited.

"I can climb the peach tree, all by myself."

"Really?" said Daddy. "I bet you're getting big."

"I am," I said. "And I'm strong too."

Daddy's voice got quiet. "You're being very brave. It must be hard to live in so many places."

"It must be hard for you to live in so many places too," I said.

Daddy gave me a kiss on the phone. It landed in my ear.

"I'll see you soon, sweetheart," he promised. "I'll see you as soon as I can."

September

I was inside my house. My new house! My new house was an apartment. An apartment for Mommy and me.

It wasn't in the city. And it wasn't in the country. It was near my old neighborhood.

I put my teddy bear on my quilt. Mommy had washed my quilt. It smelled nice and clean.

I brushed my teeth in our new bathroom.

There was a tall, skinny mirror on the back of the door. It made me look tall and skinny also.

I brushed my hair.

I tied my shoes.

My new shoes. They're red.

Then the doorbell rang. Mommy was in the kitchen.

"I'll get it!" I shouted.

We were having a party! A party for our new house.

Nana and Granddaddy Gray were at the door!

"Hi, sweetheart," said Granddaddy Gray.

Nana handed me a homemade apple pie.

"Take it to the kitchen," she said with a smile. "Don't drop it, now."

I took the pie to the kitchen. The pie

smelled very good. It smelled homey.

The doorbell rang again.

"I'll get it!" said Mommy.

"No, I'll get it!" I said. I ran past Mommy and Nana. I ran past Granddaddy Gray.

When I opened the door, Mama and Papa Brown were standing there!

"You made it!" said Mommy. She gave them a hug.

Mama Brown gave Mommy some blue-berry jam.

"We wanted to wish you luck in your new place," she said.

Papa Brown gave Mommy some vegetables from his garden. Then he gave me a big strong hug.

"How's my Ginger girl?" he said.

Mommy put fried chicken and salad and bread on the table. I went to get the

pie. Nana asked me to cut it! We filled our plates with food and started eating.

"We sure have missed Ginger," Mama Brown said to Mommy. "We can't wait until she visits us again at the farm."

"Ginger is a big help," said Papa Brown.

"We want Ginger to visit us, too," said Nana.

"We sure do," said Granddaddy Gray. Then Granddaddy Gray gave me a present. It was my very own album to put pictures in.

"Thank you," I said.

Mommy smiled at me. I felt kind of shy. Everybody was being so nice!

The doorbell rang one more time.

I jumped up and ran.

There was one more person at the door...

10
The Mystery Guest

"Daddy! Oh, Daddy!"

It was him! He'd come off the road. He had his trumpet case in his hand.

Daddy put down his trumpet. He picked me up in his arms.

"How's my girl!" he said.

I wrapped my arms around his neck. I gave him a kiss on the cheek. He had a scratchy beard, just like always.

Daddy put me down. "Hi, everyone!" he said in a loud voice. "Thought I'd stop by."

"We're glad you did," Mommy said. She winked at me. "I was saving Daddy's visit as a surprise."

"Sit down, son," said Mama Brown. "Have something to eat."

"In a minute," said Daddy. "I have someone outside who wants to come in."

"Who is it?" I asked.

"A mystery guest," he said.

He went outside. When he came back, he was carrying a little cage. The kind that people use to travel with pets.

I bent down and looked inside. Daddy unlatched the small door.

An orange cat marched out. He was big. And fat. And fluffy.

"Whose cat is that?" I asked.

Daddy smiled. "Don't tell me you don't know who he is!"

I touched the fat cat's orange fur. It

was so soft! I petted the cat's back.

The cat looked at me with big green eyes. My heart started beating fast.

"Oh!" I said. "Is it Leo?"

Daddy nodded.

"Oh my goodness!" said Mommy.

Daddy put the fat cat in my arms. The cat licked my face. And his tongue felt like sandpaper.

I held him tight. He said *meow* in my ear.

"It *is* Leo!" I said. "How did you get him?"

"The last stop on the tour was in Florida," said Daddy. "When I was there, I went to see the Cromwells."

"But he's so big!" I told him. "Leo was only a kitten."

"He grew," said Daddy.

Daddy petted Leo's fur. Then he looked at me.

"He grew. Just like you."

11
A New Day

I looked out my window.

Yellow leaves were on the ground. So many that I couldn't count them.

I saw the big blue mailbox on the corner. I saw the playground across the street.

In two more days, I would start my new school.

"Come, Leo!" I said.

Leo crawled out from under my quilt. Leo stretched and said *meow*.

"Let's go outside," I said.

I got my red kite and my big ball of string. When I dangled the string in front of Leo, he jumped!

I told Mommy we were going outside for a while.

"What are you going to do?"

"Oh, nothing," I told her.

Maybe we would fly my kite.

Or look at clouds.

Or maybe we would meet new kids!

Or new cats.

We'll play and play all day, I thought, as I left my house.

Mommy watched me from the window. I waved and she waved back.

Tonight Daddy is coming to visit. I'm going to ask him to sing that song, "Sweet Ginger Brown." Then tomorrow I'm going

to have dinner with Daddy. Daddy has a new apartment, too.

Yesterday, Leo got a postcard from the Cromwells. They wanted to keep in touch.

Mommy and I read it to him. Leo looked interested. I think that cats can remember.

The Cromwells said that Leo could come back to Florida anytime.

Leo and I have many houses.

Many houses with people.

People who love us.

People we love.

We're lucky.

DON'T MISS THE NEXT GINGER BROWN BOOK!

"Hi!" I hollered. "Who are you?"

The boy was little. Not that little, but littler than I am. He had curly hair and a striped T-shirt and dark brown skin.

A little voice came out of him: "Nobody."

Then, without another word, the boy walked away.

"What's the big idea?" I said.

He ran off into the woods.

That boy had made me mad. Who needs a Nobody Boy anyway?

From *Ginger Brown: The Nobody Boy*
by Sharon Dennis Wyeth

About the Author

Sharon Dennis Wyeth knows what it's like to move into new houses. When she was a little girl, her parents got a divorce—just like Ginger Brown's parents. But her family's love and support helped her get through that very confusing time.

"My grandparents were the calm centers in the storm," Ms. Wyeth says. "They had two ready-made homes for me. Even during that difficult period, I felt very special."

Ms. Wyeth lives with her husband, Sims, and daughter, Georgia, in New Jersey.